Spider School

Francesca Simon
Illustrated by Tony Ross

Orion
Children's Books

First published in Great Britain in 1996
by Orion Children's Books
This edition first published in Great Britain in 2010
by Orion Children's Books
a division of the Orion Publishing Group Ltd
Orion House
5 Upper Saint Martin's Lane
London WC2H 9EA
An Hachette UK Company

1 3 5 7 9 10 8 6 4 2

The Orion Publishing Group's policy is to use papers that
are natural, renewable and recyclable products and made
from wood grown in sustainable forests. The logging and
manufacturing processes are expected to conform to the
environmental regulations of the country of origin.

A catalogue record for this book is available from the British Library.

ISBN 978 1 4440 0145 7

Printed in China

www.orionbooks.co.uk

For my mother, Sondra,
a teacher who has never worked
in a Spider School

Contents

Chapter 1

Kate sat up in bed.
It was thc first day of school.

"I don't want to go to a new school," said Kate.

"I don't.

I don't.

I don't."

Kate felt **SO** cross and crabby
that she did something she
had never done before.

She got out of bed
on the wrong side.

Kate looked at the clock.
Nine o'clock.
She was going to be late.

Where oh where was Mum?

Chapter 2

Mum ran into the room. "Hurry up and get dressed, Kate!" she shouted. "You'll be late for school!"

Kate ran to the wardrobe.

Her new school clothes were

gone.

Her new school shoes were

gone.

Her new school socks were

gone too.

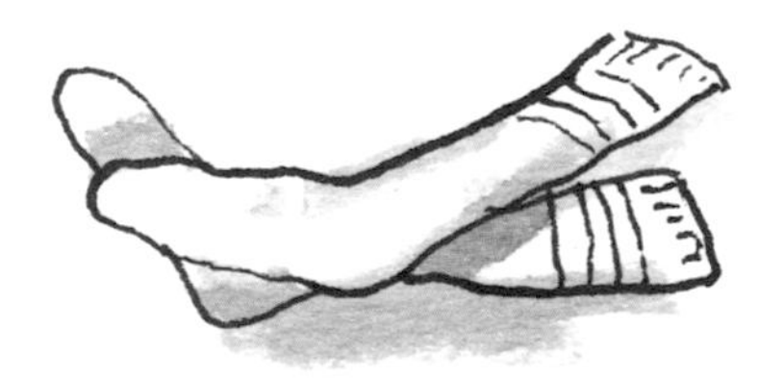

"Where are my new school clothes, Mum?"

"Gone," said Mum. "You'll have to wear something else."

Kate had to wear a dirty old skirt. Her old socks kept falling down. Her old shoes were too tight and squeezed her toes.

"Come on, Kate!" said Mum.

They ran down the street.
The street was empty.

Kate's feet thudded on the pavement.

CLUNK-CLUNK

CLUNK-CLUNK

CLUNK-CLUNK

Then Kate saw her school.

The school was big and dark and ugly.

It did not look like a nice school.
It looked like a dungeon.
Mum left Kate at the gate.

Chapter 3

"Go to Class 3," Mum said.
"But where is Class 3?" asked Kate.
"You're a big girl. You'll find it,"
said Mum.

Kate wandered up the hall.

Kate wandered down the hall.

She found

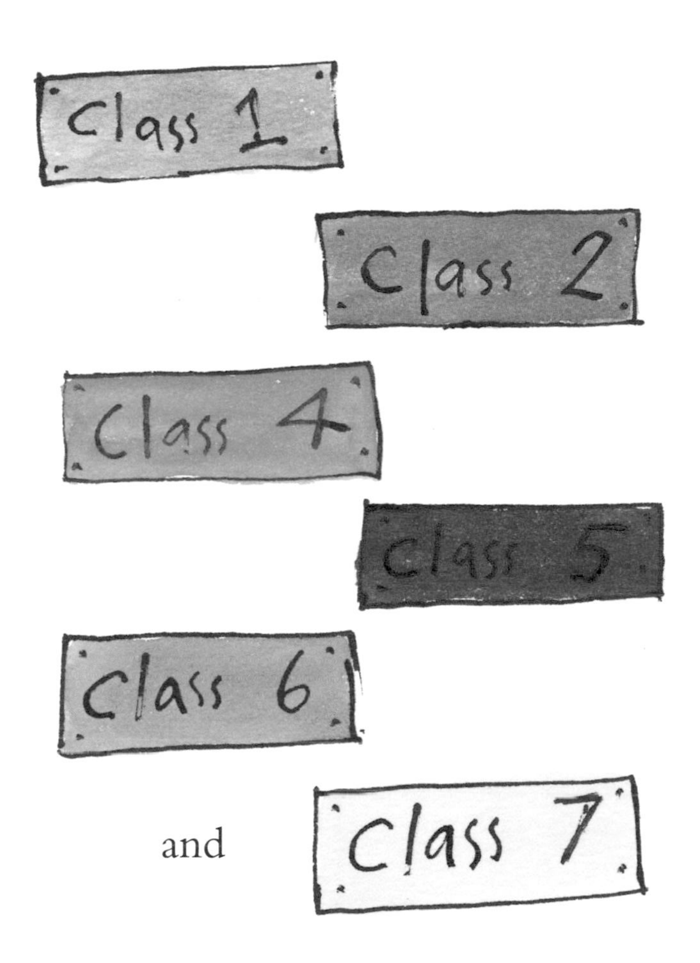

But not Class 3.

The other children hurried past her.
Everyone knew where they
were going.

But not Kate.

At last she found Class 3.
The door was very big.

Kate knocked.

No one came.

Kate knocked again, a little harder.

Still
no one came.

Kate knocked on the door
as hard as she could.

The door opened.

It was a gorilla.

“You’re late,” said the gorilla.

“But where is my teacher?” said Kate.

"I'm your teacher, stupid,"
said the gorilla.

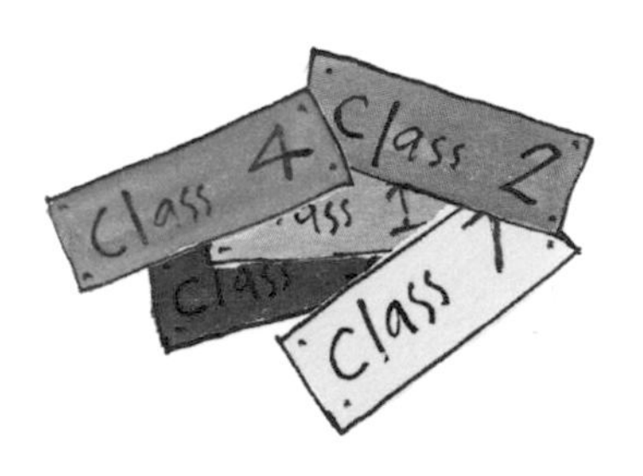

Chapter 4

All the children stared at Kate
as she tiptoed into the classroom.
She looked everywhere for her friend
Robbie, but he wasn't there.

Kate looked round the room.
The children were sitting on
the floor.

There were **no** tables.

There were **no** chairs.

There were **no** pencils.

There were **no** worksheets.

There were **no** trays.

There were **no** posters.

"Where are the books?" asked Kate.

"No books here,"

snapped the gorilla.

The children sat still.
No one said a word.

The gorilla sat at her desk
and read a comic.

Something is **not right**,
thought Kate.
She raised her hand.

"Yes?" said the gorilla.

"Where are the toilets?" asked Kate.

"No toilets at this school,"

said the gorilla.

The clock ticked loudly.

The children sat.

The gorilla read her comic.

Kate raised her hand.

"Yes?" said the gorilla.

"What are we going to learn today?" asked Kate.

"You want to learn?" said the gorilla. "Okay. What's the first letter of the alphabet?"

"A,"
said Kate.

"Wrong,"
said the gorilla.

"The first letter of the alphabet is
Z.
Now be quiet. I'm busy."

Something is **very wrong**,
thought Kate.

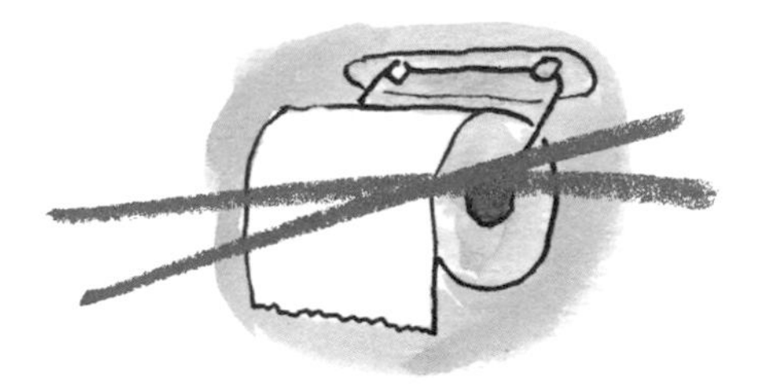

Chapter 5

The clock struck twelve.
Dinner time.
The dinner lady stood behind
a big pot.

Inside the pot were snakes
and snails and spiders.

"Excuse me," said Kate.

"Yes?" snarled the gorilla.

"I don't like snakes and snails
and spiders," said Kate.

"Oh yes you do,"
said the gorilla.

"Oh no I don't,"
said Kate.

"We don't like

and

and

shouted the children.

“Oh yes you do,”
shouted the gorilla.

“Oh no we don’t,”
shouted the children.

“I won’t eat them,”
said Kate.

“We won’t eat them,”
shouted the children.

“But these spiders are delicious,”
said the dinner lady.
“And so good for you.
Try one with tomato sauce.”
She popped a spider
into her mouth.

“Delicious,” said the dinner lady.
“Try one, Kate.” And she dangled
a big black spider in front of her.

Kate screamed.
"I don't want a spider! I don't want to be at this horrible spider school!
I want to go home!"

Chapter 6

Kate ran home as fast as she could.

She ran to her bedroom, took off her clothes, put on her pyjamas, jumped into bed, pulled the duvet over her head and closed her eyes.

Then Kate sat up, took a deep breath, and got out of bed.

But this time she got out on the **right** side.

The sun was shining.
Mum peeped in at the door.
"Am I late for school?" asked Kate.
"No," said Mum.
"It's only seven o'clock."

Kate felt very happy.

She put on her new school clothes,

ate breakfast,

and walked to school with Mum.

Kate's teacher met them at the door. "Hello, Kate, welcome to our school," said her teacher. "I'm Mrs Gillitt."

Class 3 was lovely and bright. There were tables and chairs. There were pencils and worksheets and a tray for Kate. And there was her friend Robbie, reading in the corner.

"Here's the cloakroom,
where we hang our coats and hats,"
said Mrs Gillitt.

"And here are the toilets."

And the school dinner?
Kate had peas, carrots, chips
and chicken.

No snakes, no snails,
no spiders . . .

Well, hardly any.